Beacon the Magical Dolphin

Written by
Jess Johnson

Illustrated by
Maggie Flavhan

To my wife and son, Lorraine and Ryan.

Thank you for all the wonderful experiences

we have shared on the water.

This book was only possible because of you.

THE FLORIDA KEYS HAS ALWAYS BEEN A MAGICAL PLACE. FOR THE PAST FEW YEARS, THREE YOUNG DOLPHIN CALVES PLAYED TOGETHER IN THE BEAUTIFUL TURQUOISE WATERS AND BECAME GREAT FRIENDS. THEY WOULD SPEND THEIR DAYS FEEDING ON SCHOOLS OF SMALL FISH AND AN OCCASIONAL LOBSTER.

THEY WOULD PLAY IN THE WAVES AND THE WAKES CREATED BY THE BOATS NAVIGATING THE WATERS AROUND THE MANY ISLANDS. FROM TIME TO TIME THE YOUNG DOLPHIN WOULD FLIP AND SPIN OUT OF THE WATER DOING TRICKS FOR SOME OF THE FISHERMEN.

ONE DAY THE THREE YOUNG DOLPHIN WERE SEARCHING AMONG THE CORAL FOR FOOD WHEN ONE OF THEM LET OUT A HORRIFIC SCREAM. THE SMALLEST OF THE THREE HAD CHASED A LOBSTER INTO ONE OF THE MANY DARK HOLES IN A REEF AND HAD BEEN BITTEN BY A HUGE ELECTRIC EEL.

THE YOUNG DOLPHIN RACED BACK AND FORTH SHAKING HIS HEAD AND THEN WENT SPINNING OUT OF THE WATER FIFTY FEET IN THE AIR. WHEN HE CAME BACK DOWN AND HIT THE SURFACE OF THE WATER, THERE WAS A BRIGHT FLASH. IT WAS SO BRIGHT THAT HIS TWO FRIENDS HAD TO COVER THEIR EYES WITH THEIR FINS.

FROM THAT DAY FORWARD, THE YOUNG DOLPHIN'S BODY EMITTED THIS BRIGHT BLUE LIGHT AND HE COULD SWIM AT SPEEDS FASTER THAN ANY OTHER DOLPHIN. WHEN KING NEPTUNE, GOD OF THE SEAS, SAW THIS DOLPHIN EMITTING THIS BLUE LIGHT, HE NAMED HIM "BEACON."

AS KING NEPTUNE WATCHED THE THREE FRIENDS PLAYING, HE NOTICED THAT ONE OF BEACON'S FRIENDS KEPT BOBBING UP AND DOWN OUT OF THE WATER LOOKING AROUND TO SEE IF HE COULD SEE BOATS IN THE AREA. KING NEPTUNE THOUGHT HE LOOKED LIKE A BUOY BOBBING UP AND DOWN SO THAT'S HOW "BUOY" GOT HIS NAME.

THE THIRD DOLPHIN, THE BIGGEST OF THE THREE, WAS ALWAYS HUNGRY. THIS DOLPHIN CONTINUOUSLY TUGGED AT BUOY'S TAIL IN AN EFFORT TO GET HIM TO GO BACK DOWN TO THE REEF TO FIND SOME MORE FOOD. THAT IS HOW "TUG" GOT HIS NAME.

BEACON, BUOY, AND TUG WERE THE BEST OF FRIENDS. THEY CONTINUED TO PLAY AMONG THE WAVES AND WAKES. FROM TIME TO TIME, BEACON AND HIS FRIENDS WOULD SEE BOYS AND GIRLS ON BOATS FISHING WITH THEIR PARENTS. THE DOLPHIN WOULD JUMP OUT OF THE WATER TO ENTERTAIN THEM.

MANY OF THE PARENTS WOULD TAKE PICTURES OF BEACON, BUOY, AND TUG AS THEY
SPENT THEIR DAYS PLAYING TOGETHER IN THE BEAUTIFUL WATER IN THE FLORIDA KEYS.

ONE STORMY NIGHT THE THREE FRIENDS WERE GETTING READY TO GO TO SLEEP WHEN THEY HEARD A MOTORBOAT PASS ABOVE THEM. BUOY POPPED UP OUT OF THE WATER TO SEE WHY THE BOAT WAS OUT IN THE STORM.

BUOY NOTICED TWO LITTLE BOYS ON THE BOAT CRYING. THEIR MOTHER WAS TRYING TO COMFORT THEM AS THEIR FATHER WAS LOOKING AT A MAP. APPARENTLY THE FAMILY HAD GOTTEN LOST IN THE STORM.

BUOY DOVE DOWN TO THE REEF AND TOLD BEACON AND TUG ABOUT THE BOAT ABOVE THEM. THE THREE FRIENDS SWAM UP TO THE SURFACE TO SEE IF THEY COULD HELP.

AS THEY REACHED THE SURFACE, BEACON JUMPED OUT OF THE WATER AND LIT UP THE SKY. AS BEACON HIT THE SURFACE, HE STARTED TO SWIM NORTH TOWARDS THE MAINLAND.

THE FAMILY WATCHED AS THE BLUE STREAK CUT THROUGH THE WATER AND THEIR BOAT STARTED TO MAGICALLY MOVE TOWARDS THE LIGHT. ONE OF THE BOYS LOOKED DOWN AND SAW TUG PULLING THE BOAT TOWARDS THE LIGHT.

THE FATHER STARTED THE ENGINE AND STARTED DRIVING SLOWLY TOWARDS THE LIGHT AS THE OTHER TWO DOLPHIN SEEMED TO BE GUIDING THEM TOWARDS THE LIGHT.

IT WAS ONLY A FEW MINUTES WHEN ONE OF THE BOYS YELLED TO HIS FATHER THAT HE COULD SEE LIGHTS FROM THE SHORE. IT WAS THEN THAT THE FAMILY REALIZED THAT THE DOLPHIN HAD GUIDED THEM OUT OF THE STORM TO SAFETY.

THE MOTHER TOOK PHOTOS AS BEACON, BUOY, AND TUG JUMPED OUT OF THE WATER SPLASHING AROUND THE BOAT AS THE BOYS WAVED.

THE FATHER CUPPED HIS HANDS AND PUT THEM TO HIS MOUTH AS HE YELLED **THANK YOU** TO THE THREE DOLPHIN AS THEY SWAM AWAY AND THE BLUE LIGHT FADED IN THE DISTANCE.

AFTER THAT NIGHT WORD SPREAD THROUGH THE ATLANTIC ABOUT A MAGICAL BLUE
DOLPHIN THAT GUIDES BOATERS TO SAFETY. BEACON, BUOY, AND TUG CONTINUED TO HELP
LOST SAILORS AND FISHERMEN, AND THE TALE OF THE BRIGHT BLUE DOLPHIN GREW.

NOW WHENEVER A BOAT IS IN DANGER, THE CAPTAIN WILL LOOK ACROSS THE HORIZON SEARCHING FOR A BRIGHT BLUE LIGHT. MAGICALLY BEACON, BUOY, AND TUG WILL APPEAR AND LEAD THE BOATS TO SAFETY.

The End